Lindsay MacRae

How to Avoid
Kissing Your
Parents in Public

Illustrated by Steven Appleby

PUFFIN

For Francis

PUFFIN BOOKS

Published by the Penguin Group
Penguin Books Ltd, 80 Strand, London WC2R 0RL, England
Penguin Group (USA) Inc., 375 Hudson Street, New York, New York 10014, USA
Penguin Group (Canada), 90 Eglinton Avenue East, Suite 700, Toronto, Ontario,
Canada M4P 2Y3 (a division of Pearson Penguin Canada Inc.)
Penguin Ireland, 25 St Stephen's Green, Dublin 2, Ireland (a division of Penguin Books Ltd)
Penguin Group (Australia), 250 Camberwell Road, Camberwell, Victoria 3124, Australia
(a division of Pearson Australia Group Pty Ltd)
Penguin Books India Pvt Ltd, 11 Community Centre, Panchsheel Park,
New Delhi – 110 017, India
Penguin Group (NZ), cnr Airborne and Rosedale Roads, Albany, Auckland 1310,
New Zealand (a division of Pearson New Zealand Ltd)
Penguin Books (South Africa) (Pty) Ltd, 24 Sturdee Avenue, Rosebank,
Johannesburg 2196, South Africa

Penguin Books Ltd, Registered Offices: 80 Strand, London WC2R 0RL, England

www.penguin.com

First published in Puffin Books 2000
Published in this edition 2006
This edition published exclusively for Nestlé breakfast cereals

1

Text copyright © Lindsay MacRae, 2000
Illustrations copyright © Steven Appleby, 2000
All rights reserved

The moral right of the author and illustrator has been asserted

Set in Baskerville MT
Printed in England by Clays Ltd, St Ives plc

British Library Cataloguing in Publication Data
A CIP catalogue record for this book is available from the British Library

ISBN-13: 978-0-141-32163-9
ISBN-10: 0-141-32163-6

Contents

Family Tree

My sister's mother's
husband's brother's
nephew's sister's
brother's . . . ME!

My Dad

Neck nuzzling
 Crossword puzzling
  Ear picking
   Towel flicking
    Mum snogging
     Bog hogging
      Loud snoring
       Can be boring
        Silly laughing
         Aaarf aarfing
          Shopping getting
           List forgetting
            Football playing
             Chore delaying
              Slightly greying

DAD!

Robot Mum

It never gets cross if you're messy
It picks up your rubbish and toys
If it sees a sad film on the telly
It won't make a snuffling noise

It's got a device to make pancakes
And another to polish your shoes
It will sweep up your crumbs from the carpet
Without ever blowing its fuse

It shampoos the dog in a jiffy
It does all your homework as well
And never lets on to the teacher
You programme it so it won't tell

It makes you whole cities from Lego
Sorts out your socks into pairs
It will cook you a bowl of spaghetti
The same time as cleaning the stairs

But its kisses are cold and metallic
It can't give you hugs if you're glum
It never says how much it loves you
I think I prefer my 'real' mum.

Grandad's Lost His Glasses

Grandad's lost his glasses
He thinks they're by his bed
We're far too mean to tell him
That they're perched upon his head.

My Granny Is in Love with That Weird Weather Forecaster on the Six o'Clock News

She dreams
        that he sweeps
                her away
                        in her slippers

They dance
        through the night
                then she cooks
                        him some kippers.

It Wasn't Me, It Was Him!

There's a hole in the window
A mess on the floor
And only one cake left
Where once there were four, plus
The fish in the toilet
Is hard to ignore

But it wasn't me, it was him.

The dog had a trim
With a blunt pastry cutter
Now he's wearing your nightie
And looks like a nutter
Your keys magically
Disappeared down the gutter

But it wasn't me, it was him.

The budgie flew off
Said it needed some space
And doesn't Gran always
Stick gum to her face?
And surely a carpet's
Not hard to replace

But it wasn't me, it was him.

The toothpaste was switched
With the glue meant for tiling
It sets really quickly
Now everyone's smiling
And the fire brigade called
 – Some mistake about dialling

But it wasn't me, it was him.

Yes, I know he's a baby
Who can't leave his cot
But when your back's turned
He gets up to a lot
Let him try and deny it
I bet he cannot

IT WASN'T ME, IT WAS HIM!!!

Tricky Vicky

My pet-mad kid sister Vicky
has a nervous newt named Nicky;
rat called Ricky;
mouse called Mickey;
plus a stick-insect who's Sticky.

Dicky,
so you might have thought
would be the name of the dog she bought.
But the strange and fickle Vicky
calls the tiny terrier . . . Dave.

Mum Expects

There's a baby in my mummy's tum
It looks just like a sprout
I'm not sure how it got in there
Or how it's getting out.

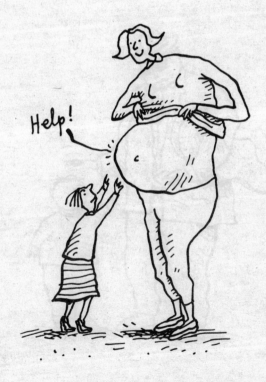

The Godfather

He makes me an offer
I can't refuse.
A ticket to Chelsea
To cheer on The Blues.

The Godfather (Part II)

He met me at my christening
When I was small and slimy.
He nearly dropped me in the font
The vicar shouted 'Blimey!'

How Was School?

Mum can't see why it's uncool
To ask me cheerfully
'How was school?'
She shakes her head and rolls her eyes
To all of the following replies:

'All right
Not bad
You what?
OK
It went
It was
Couldn't really say
It's dust
It's over
History
Stop nagging will you
What's for tea?
Same stuff
The usual
Can't remember
Ask me again in mid-December
Boring
Pointless
Stupid
Grim
Did some work
Then sang a hymn.'

My mum is such a peculiar creature
She knows how school is
She's the teacher!!

Her Latest Flame

My sister drags her boyfriends home to meet us
Subjects them all to family scrutiny
They disappear for hours up in her bedroom
Then disappear for ever after tea

Where love's concerned, Ella is like a Mountie
Fierce and direct, she always gets her boy
Dad says that she's a 'shameless little hussy',
Dumping each suitor like a broken toy

Ella can't see what we all find so funny
Boys are like fish to her, there's plenty more
Love is a game to girls like Ella
Perhaps it's because she's only four.

Dish of the Day

Every time Dad cooks dinner
You have to make an enormous fuss
Encouraged by Mum
Who says that he won't do it again
unless you say it's the most wonderful, delicious, remarkable,
fantastic, scrumptious, taste-bud popping, delectable feast,
You've ever clapped teeth on.
(*And* you have to volunteer for seconds.)
Whenever you swallow a mouthful
He hovers over you, asking:
'Is it all right – what do you think of it?
No really, tell me the truth!'
If you actually did tell him the truth,
that it's 'OK' or even 'Not bad',
He'd probably hit the roof
So instead you say:
'Wonderful, delicious, remarkable, fantastic, scrumptious,
taste-bud popping . . .'
And he smiles.
A kind of proud but trying not to be big-headed
Smile and goes:
'Can't you think of anything else to say?'
Until your mate (who doesn't know how weird your dad is)
And who hasn't noticed your mum kicking him under the
table and doing her goldfish face, which means:
'Keep your trap shut!'
Says:
'It's very nice, Mr Bishop. But it's only scrambled eggs.'

The Day That the Telly Broke Down

It was worse than a hurricane, worse than a war,
Worse than a finger that's stuck in a door,
Worse than the worst ever worst thing before

THE DAY THAT THE TELLY BROKE DOWN

My brother attempted to give it first aid.
We told it we loved it, its licence was paid.
We cried and we whimpered, we knelt down and prayed

THE DAY THAT THE TELLY BROKE DOWN

Our mum said, 'Don't worry, there's homework to do
Or something creative with glitter and glue
And just for a treat there's some washing-up too!'

THE DAY THAT THE TELLY BROKE DOWN

We could help with the ironing, go out for a walk,
Teach the parrot to do something other than squawk
Or do as they did in the olden days – talk!

THE DAY THAT THE TELLY BROKE DOWN

We considered the options with infinite care:
Like buy a new telly, attempt a repair
Or sit in our rooms wailing, 'Life's so unfair!'

THE DAY THAT THE TELLY BROKE DOWN

Instead we decided to visit our aunt
'Lend us your telly.' She said ''Fraid I can't.
This morning your uncle thought it was a plant
(and watered it!) so . . .

I'M AFRAID THAT THE TELLY HAS DROWNED.

The World's Most Popular Mother

My mother goes all weird
When friends come round to tea
She's always nicer to the friend
Than she ever is to me

We have to eat at table
We have to wash our hands
And have grown-up conversations
About summer holiday plans

The dog stays in the garden
'case he slobbers on the guest
And Mum says something really dumb
Like 'Have you changed your vest?'

Also she puts her phone voice on
The one she thinks sounds nice
The toilet's suddenly the 'loo'
Our house becomes a 'hice'

Before you've finished eating
She'll whisk away your plate
Then get your baby photos out
The ones you really hate

She goes all hip and trendy
Asks them, 'Who're your favourite bands?'
You watch your friend in horror
Become putty in her hands

Before you even know it
Cos they think your mum's so cool
You'll be sitting down to tea each day
With half the flipping school.

Nil Nil

I've been sent to my room.
It's really boring.
I've un-made my bed,
kicked the door in,
and counted the squares
on the child-proof flooring.
I can just hear the match
but not who's scoring
and outside the miserable rain
is pouring.
'You can come out now,' shouts Dad
I ignore him
cos inside the miserable sulk
is gnawing
But I'm too cross to read
or do a drawing
so I creep downstairs
and catch Man. U. scoring.
My heavy heart
is suddenly soaring.
Like the fans in the stands
we hold hands
and start roaring.

We leap in the air
call a truce to our warring.
So there we are roaring
hearts soaring
about scoring . . .
When the ref decides
it's offside.

The Mystery of My Sister's
School Photo

I moved my sister's photo
From the top of the TV.
She's been there for ages
And she's uglier than me.

Her shirt and tie are twisted
And her hair's a big disgrace.
It puts you off your egg and chips
Just looking at her face.

I haven't quite decided
Where I'm going to move her to.
Dad's wardrobe is a possible
But so's the downstairs' loo.

Or else beneath the sofa
Down among the crumbs and fluff.
That'll teach her not to tease me
And to borrow all my stuff.

That'll teach her not to wind me up
And teach her not to boast
That because she is the eldest
She's the one Mum loves the most.

Time-saving Tips for Parents

Dads spend time shaving their faces
Mums spend time shaving their legs
They should save the time spent shaving
Spending time in bed instead.

I'm Not a Picky Eater, But I'm Not Eating That

Stew is really foul and greasy
Pickled onions make me queasy
Can't stand apricots and cherries
Blue, black, straw and rasping berries
Loathe all veg including peas
Ditto anything with cheese

Chicken – don't like how you cook it
Liver – rather overlook it
Toast – I'd burn it
Marmite – spurn it
Butter – don't know why they churn it

Mincemeat sweet and also savoury
Things which lurk in thick brown gravy
Stuff which won't stay on your fork
Any product made from pork
Silvery fish with staring eyes
All varieties of pies

Soup – I do not like to slurp
Broccoli – it makes me burp
Hold the sauce
And stuff the stuffing
I'll just have a plate of
NOTHING!

Name Calling

My mum's expecting a baby
It's due on Christmas Day
I want to call it Jesus
Like in the nativity play.

(She said not to be so silly)

Or we could call it Santa
And dress it all in red
And put it in a stocking
At the bottom of the bed.

(She didn't think much of that either)

The names she likes are Imogen,
Felicity and Pearl
I just hope for that baby's sake
It comes out as a girl.

(Bet it's a boy though)

In which case
We'll probably just call it
Sebastian.

Granny Forgets

Forgets to turn the lock,
to clean her flat,
to pay for things in shops,
the names of her children,
the end of a
                    sentence.

Her train of thought thunders
through ghostly stations.

She blooms and withers in a moment.
Suddenly sixteen again
then not.

Pebbles thrown carelessly
against the dark window
frighten her.

She forgets how brave she once was,
curls up like a scrubbing fist
and turns the light on
to sleep.

She searches beneath her pillow
for her husband's creased photograph.
She has forgotten how his kisses felt,
but still hears him whistling
around the house.

Her tears fall silently as she
remembers sometimes
how forgetful she has got.

Always Remembering Eloise

I felt her like a bag of tricks
One perfect somersaulting laugh
I marvelled as her tiny heart
Beat brightly on the photograph

I waited for her to appear
Part best-beloved, part enemy
Not of my flesh but of my blood
My baby sister yet to be

I never got to hear her cry
Or stick a plaster on her knee
Play scary monsters in the dark
Or beat her at Monopoly

Her absence feels solid as an oak
The 'might have beens' its fragile leaves
Which tumble gently to the ground
Always remembering Eloise.

The Funeral

Everyone is silent in the huge black car.
A cloud full of swallowed tears
gliding two feet above the ground
towards a storm.

We're trying to be brave.
Mum holds my hand tightly.
Her fingers are like clothes pegs
clinging to washing
in a force 9 gale.
'You're hurting me,' I say.
She lets me go –
a forgotten balloon
and smiles a smile from far away,
like a smile in a photograph
in a place you can't quite remember.

We wait in line.
People mumble past us
trying not to catch our eyes.
I look at the coffin
and try to imagine Granny inside.
Can she hear me singing?
I'm singing really loudly so she'll hear.

Is she in heaven yet?
Still old and in pain?
Or whirring swiftly backwards
like a rewound tape
which pauses
at your very favourite bit.

Are hosts of heavenly angels
even as we sing
loosening her tight grey perm
and itchy curls?
Making the hair flow
like a coppery stream
down her strong young back.

I wonder if she'll wear
her tartan slippers
to dance on the clouds.

Afterwards, outside,
we weave through furious rain
towards the car.
Inside and warm again,
Mum sighs
Like summer
drifting through an open window
A feather
      or a present
            from a sky-blue
                sky.

Happy Families

Mr Pill the pharmacist
Mrs Bunn the baker
Master Leak the plumber's mate
B. Grave the undertaker.

Mr Blast, who in the past
once mended broken hooters
Mr Spider – web designer
Miss Take – in computers.

Ena Hurry makes strong curry
Old MacDonald farms
Mr Cue is in the theatre
Bill Ithole sells arms.

Master Void is unemployed
Reg Card – a referee
When I grow up, I worry what
my name suggests I'll be.

What kind of job might go with Robb?
I bet you think you know it.
But I'd rather rhyme than turn to crime
So perhaps I'll be a poet.

How to Avoid Kissing Your Parents in Public

1. RUN FOR IT at the first sign of a parent puckering.

2. SMILE. Look as if you don't mind, then say you feel really sick.

3. WHIRL AROUND very fast and go, 'Mwah, mwah!' so that they think they've got you when in fact they've missed.

4. DUCK so that the kiss lands just above your head.

5. ASK them to put it in your pocket before you get to school so that you can save it for later when nobody's looking.

YEUCK!!

6. NEVER clean your teeth and they won't want to

   or

7. DEMAND GARLIC with every meal and they won't want to either.

8. SAY you're doing a sponsored 'No Kissing Competition' and donate ten pence to charity for every missed kiss. (Note: This could prove to be expensive.)

9. TURN INTO A FROG. (Only resort to this if your mum doesn't believe in fairy tales.)

10. IF ALL ELSE FAILS, cling to their legs and beg them to give you a million sloppy kisses. They'll be so worried that they'll either take you to the doctor . . .

    or

NEVER KISS YOU IN PUBLIC AGAIN!

Lonely Heart

WANTED

Knight in shining armour for my mum. V. pretty, but not so v. pretty in morning.

Age (hers): N.O.Y.B.

Hobbies include: Wound dressing, cooking meals and throwing in bin, biscuit eating (to Olympic level), asking 'Do I look fat to you?', building castles (sand only).

Seeking: Non-squeamish male who can plan civil war battles, write convincing sick notes and revive hamsters and goldfish.

Would prefer: Professional footballer willing to spoil ungrateful and unruly children.

Would settle for: Someone to make Mum laugh like drain or ticklish princess.

The Men from Uncle

'Uncle' Greg Grundy rang on a Monday
Dinner on Tuesday
Flowers on Wednesday
Film on Thursday
In love Friday
Changed mind Saturday
Mum cried Sunday
That was the end of 'fickle' Grundy

'Uncle Dave' the Diamond Geezer
Tried his very best to please her
Bought us burgers, didn't tease her
Even shared his last Malteser
But used his nose to eat his peas – ugh!
That was the end of 'Diamond Geezer'

'Uncle' Bill was really thick
Had a heart of gold and a brain of brick
And a laugh like a gerbil who's just been sick
'Uncle' Bill got the flick quite quick

'Uncle' Sid we do not mention
Let's just say he drew a pension

Our mum is cool
But her taste in men
Leaves a lot to be desired
Plus a lot again.

What the Dog Really Thinks

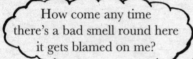

How come any time there's a bad smell round here it gets blamed on me?

Phwoar!
Look at the tail on her!

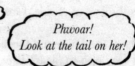

Stop going on about getting a cat to keep me company. I'm fine on my own, thank you very much, and cats stink!

Beats me why I have to turn around twenty times before going to sleep. All it does is make me feel dizzy.

Fetch!
Can't we just this once play Scrabble instead?

37

The Auntie with a Kiss Like a Heat-seeking Missile

Auntie Enid loves to kiss
Seldom does she ever miss.

Uncle 'Wet One'

Uncle Gordon puckers up
It's not so much
A kiss
He gives you as
A slippery suck

It's yuck

So if you see Gordon
Avoid him.

Please, Mum (I'm Begging You!)

Don't leave lipstick on my cheek
All my friends think I'm a freak
And Willy isn't what I'm called
I'm Bill now, middle-aged and bald.

My Sister Turned into Barbie

My sister turned into Barbie
It happened in the night
By breakfast she had gone all stiff
And her skirt was much too tight

She started wearing pink a lot
And silly purple pumps
Where once a vest covered her chest
She now had plastic lumps

Her hair became a flaxen rope
Which hung down to her knees
Her knickers they were welded on
So she couldn't go for pees

She started hanging out with Ken
Blew bubbles from her head
We had to straighten out her limbs
To get her into bed

Life was becoming a pink plastic nightmare so . . .

We took her to the toy shop
When she turned weird under water
My mum said: 'Take this flipping thing
And give me back my daughter!'

Boy and Superman

My brother's going to be Superman
When he is all grown up
He'll be too busy flying around
To do the washing-up.

Uncle Bill's Christmas

Miserable Uncle Bill
Is almost permanently ill.
And though he's neither weak nor old,
He suffers from a perpetual cold.
Having no other family near,
He comes for Christmas every year.
He lies on the sofa in his room,
A spectacle of seasonal gloom.
His presents suck. Poor mum gets grief.
The rest of us get handkerchiefs.
His sole idea of Yuletide fun
Is asking 'May I borrow one?'
Then up to his nose he brings your gift
And sucks back a tremendous sniff
Followed by a blow so loud
It's audible as far as Stroud.
Imagine then, our glad Yahoos
When we received the following news –
'I'll have to cancel I'm afraid.
I'm spending Christmas where I'm paid
To bring up phlegm and let out sneezes –
A lab which investigates diseases.
And lest you think I am unkind,
I've sent you something to remind
You all, I'm a generous Christian soul:
Some cough drops and a toilet roll.'

The Long Goodbye

I'm off then
I'm leaving
Excuse me
I've just said
I'M LEAVING!
I'm bored
Of being ignored
I'M GOING
Not sure where exactly
Just anywhere but here.
Look I'm serious you know
I'm actually going to go
Got my bag packed and everything
Got my toothbrush
Got a torch in case of emergencies
Got a load of cash
(in ten pence pieces).
Bye then
Cheerio
I've gotta go
I'm going NOW
I really, really mean it
I'm actually going
I've got my coat on
I'M GOING
I'm opening the door
Don't try and stop me
I'm going
I said

I'm **REALLY** going now
I'm **REALLY**
         ACTUALLY
               FINALLY . . .
Right, that's it!
I'm **OFF!**
I'm slamming the door behind me
I'm slamming it again
(in case you didn't notice the first time)
What the heck
One more time for luck
I've . . .
GONE

I'm out the door
        through the gate
                up the street
                        round the corner
I'm in the big wide world.
You wouldn't believe
how heavy fifteen pounds in ten pence pieces is
But I'm strong.
Right then
        I'm on my way
                On the road
                    On my own

It's raining

Perhaps I'll just phone
To tell them I'm OK
Perhaps I'll just nip back

44

To see how they're coping
Only joking.
It's raining
It's **REALLY, REALLY, RAINING**
I'm **REALLY COLD**
I'm **SOAKING!**
That does it!
I'm going home!
Next time I'll do it properly,
Pick a nice sunny day
in twelve years' time.
I'm back!
I said, **I'M BACK!**

Did anyone miss me?

Grandma Flynn

The chief pursuits of Grandma Flynn
Are keeping pets and drinking gin
And if a handsome youth walks by
She still gets a twinkle in her eye.
Determined that she will never be
A dull and boring OAP
She's full of mischief and engaged
Leading a dissolute old age.
One cannot imagine her sighing 'Dearie,
Let me sit down, I'm feeling weary'.

Last Tuesday, at about half four,
We had a policeman at the door
Asking politely if we knew
A woman arrested at the zoo –
She'd been spotted shinning up a fence
Clearly under the influence –
Grey curly hair, about five three
Attempting to set a lion free.
We followed the PC to the station
Curious to hear Gran's explanation.

Imagine our horrified surprise
At the strange scene which met our eyes –
Gran, with a cell-mate on each knee
Drunk as a lord, demanding 'Tea!'
From a sergeant who seemed happy
To 'make it hot and make it snappy'.
She held her audience in thrall
With tales from her past and stories tall
Yet still with an element of truth
Of what she'd got up to in her youth.
The laughing sergeant roared 'Tush, tush
You're enough to make a policeman blush!'

Soon they were making such a noise
That several others of the boys
In blue came down intent to see
The cause of such hilarity.
But as soon as they entered the dark cell
They too fell under Grandma's spell
Who produced from her underclothes some gin
Then shrieked 'Now the party can begin.'
This is the reason why, in short,
Ten coppers ended up in court
Charged with disorder and affray
And leading a pensioner astray.

The poor officers were sent to jail
While Grandma Flynn got off with bail,
Mainly because she lodged a plea
Of hardship and senility.
When asked by the judge, at her great age,
Why she'd been in the lion's cage,
Had it been her intent to steal
The beast, or to be its final meal.
Grandmother tearfully explained
In soft tones by emotion strained
'M'lud, on the pension that I get
I couldn't afford another pet.'

The Sight of Parents Kissing Is Very Well Worth Missing

Do you have to do that?
You're not teenagers after all.
You're blocking up the hall
or else sprawled
on the sofa.
Frankly I don't think it's on
for people with three children
to go on kissing for so long.
It's wrong!
And you look nothing like
a pair of fluffy bunnies to me.
She might be your 'sweety-darling'
but she's also 'Mum'.
Put her down please!
We know where she's been
– hoovering under the beds
and unblocking the loo –
How can you still fancy someone
who
does the kind of stuff that she has to do?
You've made her all red in the face
and she's made you
all gooey-eyed.
Parents shouldn't act like this
in fact no one should
who's over twenty-two.

The Bigg Family

Catherine, Jessica and Barry,
Edith, Enid, Anne, Bob, Harry,
Tom, Petunia and Rose,
Ian (I'm sure we've one of those).
Janice, John, Jacinta, Paul,
Philip, Fern . . .
I think that's all.
Because there are nineteen of us
Mum's sold the car
And bought a bus.

A Bigg Family Christmas

When there's nineteen of you
you have to use your imagination
and a fair amount of glue
to make enough presents to go round.
Or else you just buy each other
small things for under a pound.
Which give as much pleasure
as vastly expensive, electronic treasure.
What's also nice is . . .
we never have a turkey crisis.
Turkey in our house
doesn't end up left over
and eventually given to a dog called Rover.
We never have left-overs of anything
and we don't have a dog called Rover either.
We have a cat called Beaver
because he likes water.
(But that's another poem.)
And if you hate stuffing,
at least eight other people
will try and grab it off your plate.
We never play board games after dinner.
It takes too long to find out
who's the winner.
Instead we play netball
or soccer with nine-a-side
or else sardines.
Though it's quite hard to hide
eighteen giggling people.
Have you tried?

Quiet Please, Tom Bigg Is Dreaming

Tom Bigg dreams
                of being alone.
Of spreading his dreams
Across the empty bedroom floor
Knowing they'll still be there tomorrow
Not stolen, trampled on or borrowed.

Tom Bigg dreams
                he's been left in peace
Of reaching the end of
a sentence.
Of long, lingering baths
Which shrivel the tips of his fingers.

Tom Bigg dreams
                he's an only child
That people say:
'Isn't he polite?',
When out of the kindness of his solitary heart
He offers them a sweet.

Tom Bigg dreams
                that no one can hear him
Talking in his sleep.

When Grandad Was Young

'I had two pairs of shoes
(One for everyday and one for best)
The best ones only came out on Sundays
I would have to stuff my feet into them
Curl them up like fists 'til they burnt and hurt so much
That I'd end up walking to church on my hands

When I was young . . .
Vegetables were a luxury
Carrots were not all the same size
They were knobbly, covered in dirt
And resembled wizened old people
You didn't much like

When I was young . . .
You could have bread and butter
Or bread and jam – never both
Tangerines only appeared at Christmas
At the bottom of a very sweaty sock
With toenails in it

When I was young . . .
We played out in the street
Until we had so many scabs on our knees
That we'd have to go indoors
And pick them off while we listened to the wireless

My idea of luxury
Was a pickled egg

The fashionable thing to wear
Was a scratchy jersey
Which had such tight sleeves
That your hands would turn blue
And threaten to drop off

Our idea of fun
Was to laugh at each other's jumpers
And take bets on whose hands
Would drop off first.'

Every Other Weekend

The bell rings
And we line up in the hall
Handover time,
With me, the slippery ball.

I watch them smiling
See it's all pretend
Hard to believe they used to be in love
These days, they're barely even friends
They must have been happy once
But when?
Every other weekend.

Two sets of clothes,
Two Christmases, two rooms
I've lost count of 'Goodbyes'
And 'See you soons'.
Two separate houses
Fifty miles apart
The motorway between
A calculated silence in the dark.

My life feels like
One long confusing sum.
I love my dad
I also love my mum.
Asleep on the journey
Safe in my dreams I spend
Time with an undivided family
Each weekend.

Father's Day

It's about eating ice cream
                        mainly –
In silent, sodden parks;
On hard soaking benches;
Beneath miserable dripping trees.

It's about eating ice cream
                        mostly –
In hot choking cafes
Where the windows have steamed up
Because of the rain outside
And nervous people smoking.

It's about eating ice cream
                        usually –

In an empty cinema.
Watching a film
You've already seen
With your mum and her boyfriend.
But you don't tell him that
And anyway, it's better than the park.

It's about eating ice cream
                        really –
As he wanders the streets with you
                              weeping.
And you'd like to weep too
But you can't.
And you wonder if he knows
That it's impossible
                   to cry
And eat ice cream
At the same time.

The Sound of Silence

Downstairs
they're throwing words about.
Sharp, spat-out, vicious ones
designed to cut.
Sometimes there's an angry pause.
A door slams shut.
Full stop
then not, as another spiteful sentence
limbers up.
Someone is crying now.
The argument
collapses in a strangled sob.
Slowly I take my fingers
from my ears.
Shut off
the tense, repeating song.
Peace
is a heartbeat
drumming in my head
De-dum, de-dum, de-dum.
Not words at all
just blunt, soft thuds.

Who's a Big Boy Then?

Every so often he'll whine:
'How long, *now* until my birthday?!'
And Mum will reply wearily:
'Only 360 to go now, darling'
Then, when there's only:
'Ten more to go now, darling'
He starts bawling
about what presents he wants,
who he wants to invite to his party and –
'Can I have a fancy dress one?
Please, please!
And will you make me a cowboy outfit
and a cake, a chocolate one with my name on it
and it's got to have candles!'
And Mum says:
'All right, darling. But you'll have to help me out,
You go and buy the candles.'
So he goes down to the shop, all by himself,
and comes back with exactly thirty-nine candles
and Mum says:
'Good try, darling.
But you're one candle short
of a birthday.'

Can We Go Home Now Please?

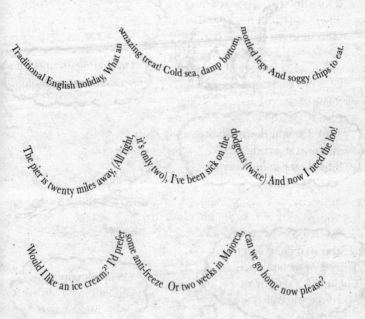

Traditional English holiday, What an amazing treat! Cold sea, damp bottom, mottled legs And soggy chips to eat.

The pier is twenty miles away, (All right, it's only two), I've been sick on the dodgems (twice) And now I need the loo!

Would I like an ice cream? I'd prefer some anti-freeze Or two weeks in Majorca, can we go home now please?

What the Cat Really Thinks

63

Summer Camp Clothing List

1 anorak
1 bobble hat
(Get real, Mum,
I'm not wearing that!)
2 jumpers, both of them too big
Some slippery soap
1 guinea-pig
Pyjamas which are much too tight
A torch to get around at night
A sweatshirt that's more sweat than shirt
A pair of boots complete with dirt
A teddy, which I'd better hide
Pants, with my brother's name inside

My stomach's tied in nervous knots
My rucksack weighs about a ton
I won't need half the stuff I've got
But think I'd better pack my mum

The Au Pair Writes a Letter Home

We have Marmite soldiers for
TEA
which is like dinner but also
a hot drink.
SOLDIERS can be men with guns
but in this meaning are
bits of cut up
toast.
TOAST are also
things on the end of your feet
or what you are making
at birthdays etc. with
glasses.
GLASSES you can drink out of
or use to see more better.

I am thinking that English
is very confusing.
But I would rather eat
the end of a person's feet
or even a real soldier
than something with Marmite
spread on it again.

The Terrible Two-year-old's Terrible Tantrum

Won't go in the car
Won't stand over there
Won't play nicely with my sister
Won't not pull her hair
Won't stop picking nose
Won't stop throwing food
Won't wait just a little minute
Won't be . . .

'Don't be rude!'

Wanna huge ice cream
Wanna drop it – splat!
Wanna dummy
Wanna bottle
Wanna wreck the flat
Wanna get my way
Want that toy – *it's mine!*
Wannit now, this very minute!

Or I'm gonna whine

Gonna cut up rough
Gonna start to scream
Gonna throw the BIGGEST TANTRUM
That you've ever seen
Gonna go for broke
Gonna start to choke
Gonna find the biggest dog

And give its eyes a poke!

Can't you lay off, Mum?
Can't you try to see
That I won't be such a monster
When I get to . . .
THREE?

The Babysitter

It was clear
From the moment
They walked out the door
That Tracey
Had never done
This job before.

Until they came home
She patiently sat
On me
      my little brother
           and the cat.

The Wicked Stepmother

I expected her to wear hobnail boots
Beneath a stiff brown skirt.
I expected her to screech
Like a throttled parrot:
'No you can't go to the ball
                               the ball'
Or:
'Scrub that floor again!'

I just knew she would offer me
Shiny, poisoned apples;
Hide all my party invitations;
Spend hours asking the mirror
Leading questions
Then take me into a forest
And leave me there.

I pictured her waiting
For the postman
To deliver a parcel
Containing my torn-out heart.

I thought I would have to
Grow my hair
Until it was long enough
To hang out of high windows

I imagined pinning all my hopes
On a mountaineering prince
Armed with a chainsaw
And a first aid manual.
Or the kindness of seven
Short men.

So imagine my surprise
When an ordinary-looking person arrived
Who likes fairy tales too.

Uncle Fred Died in Your Bed

In the dead of the night
When the clock strikes one.
The wind in the trees
Sounds like dead men's songs.
The creak in the eaves
Is a deadly surprise –
A hatchet-faced rat
Come to feast on your eyes.
Your screams can't escape,
They're stuck in your throat
And it's out on an ocean of fear
That you float.
You imagine the taxi outside
Is a hearse
It's as bad as it gets
But it's going to get worse.
For a strange-looking ghoul
Has slipped into your room
Who out-grims the Grim Reaper,
A prophet of doom.
He's got such bad dandruff
He looks like he's snowing
And as he approaches
You realize . . .
You know him!
Your mother once said
'He'd been weaned on a pickle.'
He wouldn't respond to a joke
Or a tickle.

He was cruel to all creatures,
As tight at a fist,
When he went to his grave
Well, he wasn't much missed.
The bed where you sleep
Is the bed where he died
He tells you the mattress
Has treasure inside.
As his skeletal fingers
Discover the loot
He floats up to the ceiling
And lets out a hoot.
'I didn't mind dying,' he laughs
'I was ready, but hell
Will be more bearable with my . . .
Teddy!'

Hand Me Down

Hand me down
that jumble jumper.
Hand me down
a skirt.
Hand me down
the brutal lie
That being poor
can't hurt.

Fill me up
with 'sell-by dates',
'reduced to clears' –
they're cheap.
I'll bite down
on my fingers
as I rock
myself to sleep.

Will You Be My Family?

Will you take my picture?
Will you take my side?
Will you take the pain away
I've tried so hard to hide?

Will you watch me play in goal
In foul or freezing weather?
Could we spend all Christmases
And holidays together?

Will you pack a lunch for me?
Sometimes hold my hand?
Can we be just ordinary?
Do you understand?

When I throw a tantrum
Will you promise not to pack?
If I learn to love you
Will you try to love me back?

Will we see the funny side?
Laugh when times get tough?
We will be a family
That will be enough.

I Am the Lullaby

I am the footsteps in the hall
I am the hand that wipes the tears
I am the stars that pierce the dark
I am the song that soothes all fears
I am the kiss that finds the cheek
I am the air where dreams take flight
I am the story's happy end
I am the lamp left on at night.

The Fruit Sticker Sorcerer

More of a magician
than a second dad.
When my friends ask me what he does
I say that he conjures magic from the weekly shop.
That it's like gliding with Merlin
down a supermarket aisle.
I watch him delighted from my Tesco chariot,
peeling foreign countries
from the skins of fruit.
He sticks them gently
in the tiny valleys between his knuckles
and rolls down his sleeves.
Then in the dark street afterwards,
he pulls them up again.
His arms are more crowded
than a conquering general's map.
We've taken Jamaica, Israel, Guadeloupe,
several small islands in the balmy South.
Spellbound, I watch him fill the collection book
with our hoard of treasure no one else would want.
All the exotic lands I can't pronounce
shimmer in sunlight
cast by the table lamp.

The Thingy

Shin kicker
Snot flicker
Crisp muncher
Shoulder huncher
Grudge bearer
Out starer
Back stabber
Biscuit grabber
Sock smeller
Fib teller
Thinks that it's
Uri Geller.

Loud belcher
Slug squelcher
Pillow drooler
I'm the ruler
Gonna beat yer
That'll teach yer
Bog ugly
Swamp creature
Found mainly
Undercover
What is it?

MY BROTHER!

The Bug Buster

Instead of nasty nit lotion
Combed through every lock
A new machine keeps my head clean
It comes as quite a shock.

I used to loathe the creepy-crawlers
Now I think they're fun
Cos Mum's gone down to Boots and bought
A head-louse zapping gun.

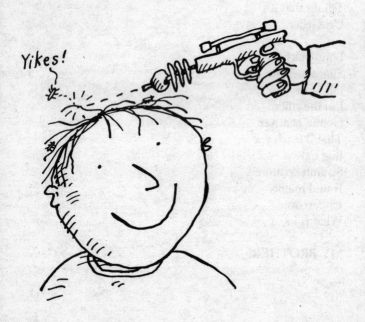

Yikes!

The Cleaner

We're frightfully rich
And out to impress
So we hire a cleaner
To clean up our mess

But because we're ashamed
Of the filth in our lives
We do all the cleaning
Before she arrives.

Seven Sides of Seven Brothers

One is the sporty one – lives in the gym
Two is the weepy one – cries so much that deep puddles
                               form around his knees
                               in which you can swim
Three is the shaggy one – he could do with a trim
Four is the fat one – also known as Slim
Five is the angry one – inclined to be grim
Six is the clumsy one – always out on a limb
Seven isn't born yet – so he's interim
Eight is the odd one out – a her not a him!

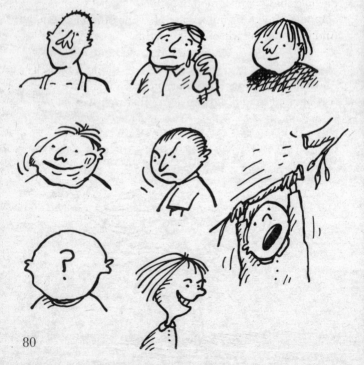

Do I Look Like an Octopus to You?

Do I look like an octopus to you?
Do I have eight hands instead of two?
Do I trail seaweed
And emit a strong whiff of fish
As I'm
Decorating a birthday cake
Prising the post from the jaws of a slobbering dog
Plunging a tentacle into the hoover bag to find the
                                        missing key
Changing a plug and the baby's nappy simultaneously
Picking slugs out of a mouldy lettuce
Scraping something unpleasant off your brother's boots
And spinning the wheel for the gerbil
                        because he's too bone idle
                                to do it himself?
All while waving my remaining sucker in your face
As I attempt to find the answer to my own question
Which is . . .
NO – I DO NOT **LOOK** LIKE AN OCTOPUS
CLEARLY, I'M A NONPLUSSED NONOPUS!

Daily Exam Paper Designed for Monosyllabic Older Brothers

1. Did you have a nice day at school?

    Err

2. Have you got much homework?

    Yer

3. Who spilt this on the sofa?

    (pointing at your sister) Her!

4. What's your new teacher called?

    (sarcastically) Sir

5. What's his name really?

    Phipps

6. What would you like for dinner?

    Chips

7. What does a bear do in the winter?

    Kips

8. What do you want for your birthday?

    Com-pu-ter

9. What's the magic word?

    Cheese?

10. What's the other one?

Please!

Good. 9/10 monosyllables. But not quite monosyllabic enough to be a stroppy teenager.

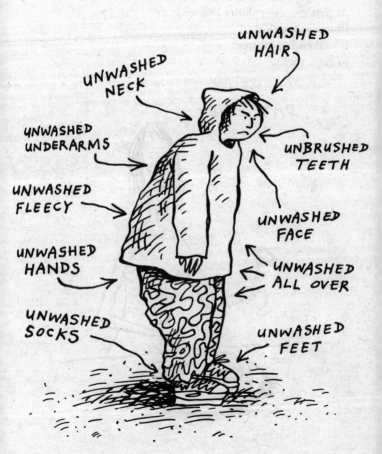

UNWASHED HAIR

UNWASHED NECK

UNWASHED UNDERARMS

UNBRUSHED TEETH

UNWASHED FLEECY

UNWASHED FACE

UNWASHED HANDS

UNWASHED ALL OVER

UNWASHED SOCKS

UNWASHED FEET

Gran's Diet Advice

Gran told my sister
that if she chews every mouthful
forty times, she'll never get fat.
At first my sister didn't believe her.
But now she does.
It's taken her all week
to eat a pizza.

DAY FIVE:

YOYDIY?

Y
O
Y
do
U
do
DIY?
Tools
R
not
U.
Leave
M
2
me
4
U
L
C
I
M
bet
R
8
8
than
U.

What the Goldfish Really Thinks

86

Look Who's Talking

You are the dog poo on my shoe!

You are the smell of unwashed socks!

You are the sound of throwing-up!

You are the itch of chickenpox!

You have the IQ of a flea!

You have the manners of a hog!

You are as mouldy as old cheese!

You are as slimy as a frog!

You are much uglier than me!!

Gotcha! It simply isn't true!
That's why we're called identical,
I am no uglier than you!

You Might As Well . . .

Small brothers blame you;
Big ones skulk;
Mothers shame you;
Sisters sulk.
Dads won't budge
Unless you shove 'em.
But they're family;
You might as well love 'em.